By Gail Herman

Illustrated by Duendes del Sur

SCHOLASTIC INC.

New York Toronto London Auckland Sydney
Mexico City New Delhi Hong Kong Buenos Aires

ISBN 0-439-24236-3

12 11 10 9 8 7 6 5 4 3 2 1 1 2 3 4 5 6

Designed by Maria Stasavage
Illustrated by Duendes del Sur

Printed in the U.S.A.
First Scholastic printing, September 2001

Fred waved a piece of paper. “But I got information in the mail. And free tickets!”

Just then a hot dog cart rolled by. Free tickets? Hot dogs?

“Like, what are we waiting for?” said Shaggy.

Suddenly the two buddies
jumped back in the van.
Shaggy's teeth chattered.
Scooby's fur stood on end.

"W-w-w-we saw something!" said Shaggy.

"What?" said Velma.

"A riant! Rig, rhite reeth!" said Scooby.

"A giant?" asked Velma. "With big white teeth?"

Everyone looked around. But nothing was there.
"Are you sure about this?" asked Velma. "Maybe you made a mistake."

“Hot dogs! Get your hot dogs. French fries! Jumbo size!” the hot dog guy called.

Scooby sniffed. “Rummy!”

“Like, maybe we did make a mistake,” said Shaggy.

A few minutes later, the gang
sat in their seats.
"Great seats," said Shaggy.
"The first race is about to start," said
Daphne.
A man stood at the starting line. He
waved a flag, and the cars took off.

7

"Wow," said Fred.
"Those drivers really go!"
The cars raced around the track, then passed the gang again.
"Check out those squealing tires!" said Shaggy.
"Rokay," said Scooby.
He leaned over the railing.

“Not so far, good buddy,” Shaggy said.

All of a sudden, an engine backfired. Shaggy and Scooby jumped in fright — right over the railing!

Thud! They fell onto a speeding car.

“Hang on!” cried Shaggy.

"Ruh-roh," Scooby cried.

There it was again. White flashing teeth. Big bloodshot eyes. It *was* a monster!

The car zoomed past.
Rrrrrr! The monster roared.
Frightened, Shaggy and Scooby shot up in the air.
Thud! They dropped back into their seats.

“Stop clowning around,” Fred said. “I’m trying to watch the race.”

“Ronster!” cried Scooby.

“We saw that thing again,” Shaggy gasped. “And it really is a monster!”

"Sure, guys," said Fred. He was watching the race. "Whatever you say."

"Did you hear us, Velma? Daphne?"

"Go, cars, go!" they shouted, excited.

Scooby and Shaggy slumped in their seats. Nobody was listening.

Then the race was over.
"Did you say something?" said Velma.
"We saw the monster again!" Shaggy cried.
"Why didn't you say so?" said Fred. "Let's investigate!"

Velma nodded. “Let’s start in the parking lot. That’s where Shaggy and Scooby saw the monster.”

“I’m not going near that parking lot,” said Shaggy.

“Re either,” Scooby said.

"Come on, guys," said Fred.

Shaggy and Scooby shook their heads.

"Please?" said Daphne.

They shook their heads harder.

"We have Scooby Snacks in the van," said Velma. "And the van is in the parking lot."

Everyone hurried to the van. Velma started throwing things out of the back.

"I have those Snacks somewhere," said Velma.

All at once, a roar thundered through the lot.

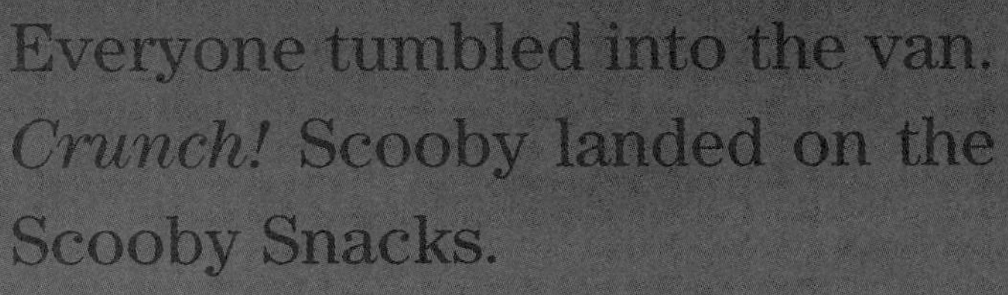

Everyone tumbled into the van.
Crunch! Scooby landed on the Scooby Snacks.
"Yum! Scooby crumbs!" said Shaggy, digging in.

RRRRRR! The monster reared up
in front of the gang.
"Zoinks!" cried Shaggy.
It stood as high as the treetops.
Sharp teeth flashed.

“Let’s get out of here!”

The Mystery Machine took off. But the monster was right behind . . . chasing them . . . getting closer!

All at once, more monsters appeared. Dozens of monsters. All different colors. All different shapes.

THE MYSTERY MACHINE

"I'm driving onto the racetrack," Fred cried. "It's the only place to go!" Velma saw the stands. People were cheering. Jinkies, she thought, that's strange.

THE MYSTERY MACHINE

Then she had an idea. She grabbed the information about the racetrack.

"Like, now you're reading?" said Shaggy. "When there are monsters chasing us?"

"They're monsters all right," said Velma. "Monster trucks!"

Velma showed everyone the
racing schedule.
"Second race: Monster trucks."
Just then they crossed the finish line.
Fred braked. Everyone got out of the van.
"See?" said Velma. "Those trucks are made up
to look like monsters. Teeth and all!"

A man came up to them, holding a trophy.
"Congratulations!" he said.
"Re ron!" said Scooby.
"Like, cool!" said Shaggy. "And we weren't even trying!"
"Scooby-Dooby-Doo!"